Annie McDo~~~

Barb Dwye~

Beastie La St~

Betsy Anders~

Bronwen John~

C E Marshall

Caroline James Mackie

Chris Tait

Daniel Duggan

Fiona Anderson

Ginny Britton

Hannah Kempton

Helen Monaghan

Lea Taylor

Liam McKnight

Liam Paterson

Kaisha Jayne

Kate Trought

Magdalena Hollingsbee

Mary Turner Thomson

May Halyburton

Mimi Sertherlon

Molly Arbuthnott

Robyn Thomson

Ross Hartshorn

Sophie Devereux

Wendy Woolfson

The Book Whisperers
community . interest . company

Introduction

The Book Whisperers are proud to present this anthology of our members work – Once Upon *Another* time. A Festive Anthology of stories, anecdotes, poems and pictures, from published and unpublished writers, from new scribblers to international best-selling authors. What makes The Book Whisperers special is the community of writers, authors, poets and illustrators, coming together to support and encourage each other – learning and growing together.

"Haven't we all done well. Look at you all, you've beavered away with your pens and paper getting your stories all lined up in time for Christmas. I'm ecstatic with this book. ONCE UPON ANOTHER TIME has something for everyone. The quality of writing is consistently good plus the range and breadth is extraordinary. Thank you for being part of The Book Whisperers wonderful book ride - we look forward to reading and sharing more of your work in future. In the meantime Slainte and Merry Christmas."

Lea Taylor, Creative Director of The Book Whisperers.

Huge thanks to those behind the scenes who go above and beyond to make it happen. Mary Turner Thomson, Mandy O'Connor and Lea Taylor. And special thanks to all those that submitted pieces for this seasonal book.

www.TheBookWhisperers.com

Contents

Move Me

ANNIE MCDONNELL

They are the poets,
our weaver of words,
collectors of thoughts.

Putting words to paper,
Sunflower fields become oceans
a touch becomes electronic light.

Then, suddenly,

The Words
Are Whispered
through the wind.

On flights of air
and become the breeze,
That lightly caresses us.

They'll bring us to attention
And even to our knees,
Weeping and loving.

They are Poets,
They fix the broken
And revere the unnoticed.

Make us see the unseen.

They remind you,
To look at the Stars,
But see them in your hands.

These wordsmiths,
Move mountains,
And hearts, and hope.

Stir Souls.

They cross
Seas, and Countries,
And continents.

The world.

They move farther
than airplanes and ships.

They can unite us.

This is why
And how
they move me.

Simple Pleasures

MOLLY ARBUTHNOTT

Once upon another time
The sky was always blue!
Everyone was laughing and asking 'how do you do'?
The world was filled with people who all put others first.
The earth was infected with such love that it almost burst!
At Christmas, communities together came.
We all existed on the same plane!
Humans, animals, plants and minerals as one
In a balance where each shone and life for all was fun!
We spoke, grew and healed each other
Mother, father, sister, brother
Perfect harmony of sun and earth
Every day began like a virgin birth.
Our actions are reflected in everything you see ...
The power for change exists in you and me.

Tinsel Dreams

BEASTIE LA STICK

author of 'Exit Strategy'

Once upon another time there were two parents. For our amusement, let's call them Cinderella and Price Charming. Together they had three beautiful children. However, one day Cinders got real tired of the Prince's nonsense. She grew insidiously bored of picking up, putting out and talking to a brick wall at numerous points of the day and so they split up.

The End.

The shortest versions can be the most honest. When we can try to not lay blame or create embellishments but sticking to the facts can become a challenge.

From August to December, Xmas was always a big, over-priced, plastic decoration to focus on when our relationship was bad. I couldn't deprive them of a 'Mum and Dad Christmas' at such a young age, could I?

At some point though, if you want to keep your sanity, you have to kick the gremlins out of your mind and begin thinking of an alternative. One where we split the festive day or even shared it as a pseudo family. After all we were still friends.

2021 will be the first Christmas of just me and the kids. For most of the day, I'm sure it'll be no different. I was always the organiser. I assumed he didn't care and so left everything to me but over time, I wonder if he trusted me to do a good job or maybe he just got sick of being told "Yes, we could do that but probably my way is better" I paraphrase. Though, I've never pretended to be perfect. I think.

Can it be the same? Of course not.
Does that matter?
Yes.
But that's fear talking.
Sometimes a tiny voice will ask, "But what about your feelings?"
As logic calms my nerves.
But aren't birthdays and Christmas' pivotal days?
The fear returns to my gut again. This time with knuckle dusters.

Vic's birthday just passed.
He was 10.
The day wasn't any different, I must confess.
I bought most of the gifts, chose the cake, wrapped up presents into the small hours before blowing up balloons with the last of my energy.

Loneliness.
I didn't realise I was lonely.
Now I have a comparison.
But that brings less comfort.

I try to think of the good times.
Building Vic's go-kart at 2am on Xmas morning in 2018.
On it's first shot, it came back in two parts.
It went in the garage and never came out again.
All the necessary screws lost in a drain near the chippie.
It's the disappointment, that's what stings.
Knowing the dream could never be.
The hope of working together, being supportive and loving.
All of those ideas are still diagrams and lists within notebooks.
None of it materialised or came wrapped in tinsel.

So why do I hold onto this with candy-cane coloured fingernails?
Avoiding the problems of intimacy, just so I could have that
annual 'Santa hat' photo of him and the kids.
Each year a tradition.
As the kids grew in numbers and in height.

That won't happen this year.
It would feel fake and untrue but then again was it ever anything
other than a Panto.

So, logistically
Do I have them on Christmas morning? Of course. I'll fight for
that.
But then I feel for him.
As he wakes up to the sound of nothing.
The family he now shares 30/70.
How did it get to this?

And then, my time later on when he takes my children away.
The death of the laughter, chatter and the endless fights.
Left to drown in a sea of wrapping paper.
Alone.

You know it's me and the bottle then.
Touching a hand over their bedding.
The pillows they wont rest on tonight.
As I dump my brokenness onto the bed and say goodnight to
Christmas day.

A Bed of Holly

ROBYN THOMSON

Blair sat with a full glass of expensive mulled wine balanced between her fingers. The room she was in was filled with festive lights, ornaments and pretty little glass trinkets that sat upon the crackling fireplace. Next to the sofa, were two large windows that acted like frames for the work of art that was the snow falling onto the slushy street below. Lowering the blanket that hugged her legs, her phone pinged — a message from her wife, Emily. The gold bracelets that sat around her thin wrist jingled as she raised the blue light to her eyes.

"Hey baby, I'm going to be late getting home, but I had the gift I got you sent straight to the house! Happy holidays my love!"

Rolling her eyes, Blair threw the phone to the pillow next to her. "Pathetic, I bet its shit." She grumbled as she got up and walked, warm wine in hand, to the table that sat against the furthest wall. Placing the glass down, she pulled the drawer open, and lifted out a small flip phone from under a pile of papers. A girlish grin appeared on her lips as she skipped back over to the couch, texting away with eagerness.

"Hey sexy thing, when you gonna be here? The misses won't be home till super late."

She paused for a moment as she watched the other person receive the message and type a reply, then the sweet vibration of response came through.

"Funny you should message me, I'm outside."

Blair stared at the text for a second before looking down the hallway. The lights in the house were all off, with only the glow of the fireplace and the strewn red and green fairy lights to see by. Getting to her feet, she fixed her hair and the short dress that clung to her thighs. She took a nearby wine bottle in hand, and walked down the hall - ignoring the wedding pictures that Emily had so lovingly framed and hung on the wall. She wrapped her bony fingers around the door handle. Opening with a creak, she looked out to see the silouette of a figure standing before her in a large red raincoat.

"That was faster than expected," Blair hummed as she pushed back the snow covered hood.

"Surprise!" Emily sang as she slipped inside, getting the side of her partner's dress wet as she went. Blair stood stunned for a moment as she watched her wife remove her jacket and walk into the living room, a large box in hand.

"What are you doing here? I thought you had to work late tonight?" Blair following Emily into the room - trying not to sound alarmed and disappointed.

"Oh, that was just a little fib to get you excited. There is no way I would miss today for the world!"

Coming over to Blair, she planted a cold damp kiss that sent chills of utter disgust down Blair's spine. "Here baby! Your present!" she chirped as she placed the large cardboard box down onto the glass coffee table. Blair looked behind her, unsure about what was going on. Worried that she would have to explain to a second guest.

"What's wrong darling," Emily said with a harsh whisper. "You weren't expecting anyone, were you?"

Blair paused for a moment and looked Emily up and down. "No, why would I be? Don't go accusing me of things now." She snapped as she sat down, looking at the soggy box. "What is it?" she groaned like a spoiled child.

Emily smiled as she leaned down to open the box for her beloved. "Holly." Lifting the lid of the box a sour smell immediately assaulted Blairs senses. There inside the box covered in cotton and dried hollies was the severed head of her mistress. Her brain leaked a thick liquid into the red berries as it sat half out of the cracked open skull. Her hair was ripped out in chunks, and a single eye dribbled out onto her cheek. The second eye was gone, leaving the socket stuffed with holly berries that fell out into the box. Blair couldn't even scream. She could only look up at her once loving wife, who stood smiling down at her.

"What's wrong sexy thing, don't like it?" she sarcastically asked as she removed the cleaver that she had hidden within her belt.

Jingle Bell Rock

BEASTIE LA STICK

author of 'Exit Strategy'

In November,
When we buy extra batteries with our weekly shop.
The feeling of 'being prepared' does wonders.

I'm not repeating the Xmas of 2011.
When 20 toys were unwrapped and only one AAA battery was
found.
Dad did his duty and jumped on a mountain bike.
A trouper.
For neither of us could legally drive on Christmas morning.
Bucks fizz, baby...
I begin drinking when I preheated the oven for the turkey.

Tipsy by 11am.
"Jingle Bell Rock!" blasts
Each year I promise to learn it's bouncy lyrics.
This year, I will.

Then the neighbours ring the bell.
Are welcomed in with open arms as they play Santa to the kids.
We open more prosecco and everyone leaves happier than
when they arrived.

I'll hold onto these memories, thank you.
There were some good times In-between the bad.
The memories of making, or should I say hashing up Mum's trifle
that at my hands turned into soup.
Mimi dressed in an unforgettable smile as she unwrapped 'Mim
Mim'.
To me, £45 for a purple rabbit teddy.
To her, pure joy in her arms.
The cynicism in my heart melts a little.
Yet, what shouldn't be unseen is the child's fingers who stitched
it.

And this year,
There will be no money in the pot for me.
But that's OK
All I want is ...
To know in my bones, that although my choices don't come gift
wrapped.
And my knees still shake.
That I haven't mastered a week without yelling.
I've got debts in corners I haven't dusted.
All I really want is ... to know that I'm a good Mum.

My brother says I am.

He's my pillar of strength, armed with mountains of positive
presents inside each of them is a reason to laugh.

Again

CAROLINE JAMES MACKIE

author of 'Lizzie, the Best Little Giant'

Christmas Eve. You'd never know. No tree, no tinsel, no star, no lights. And the cooker just wouldn't turn on either so it would be microwaved frozen pizza tonight. Again.

Ronnie had known it was going to be a rotten Christmas all month already. The whole of December was a nightmare anyway what with the shops full of stuff she wasn't getting - so what was one more night eh?

She had hoped for better this year, but when mum had her go to the foodbank the day before yesterday, again, with only a couple of days to go ... well, she knew not to go moaning about not having a tree this year, again.

Just once though, she'd like to be able to say 'again' for something nice. 'Oh, we're having roast dinner, again.' 'Can we play your favourite game again mum?' 'Shall I pour you a glass of wine ... again?' But no, it was always bad stuff that was again. Again.

Wasn't mum's fault, she knew that, but when she was laid off, again, she knew already. Christmas was going right down the pan. Third year in a row, since dad. She should have known, but you just keep hoping. She was big enough now to understand but that didn't stop her wishing. Wanting. Again.

She had a whole list of stuff she wanted, most of it for her mum, plus practical things, for school and for the house. Just 'enough in the cupboards for a whole week' would have been nice around Christmas, but, well, it wasn't to be. Again. Then the door went.

Mum got her to answer it, saved her getting out of bed and she was a mess anyway so ...

Ronnie straightened her hair and pulled open the door. Nobody there. Just a big box with a card stuck to it.

She grabbed the card and shut the door on the box, taking the card to her mum who ripped it open, then couldn't get out of bed fast enough to yank the door open and drag the heavy box inside.

An angel must have left it and the card said,

'Have a nice Christmas, from a well-wisher'

The box was stuffed with a week's worth of groceries. Everything possible! Including special Christmassy stuff and everything to make a lovely Christmas dinner, an already freshly cooked, roasted chicken included. A stocking full of little gifts for Ronnie and a selection box! Chocolates, a bottle of wine, the lot!

Ronnie's mum cried her eyes out as she hung up the streamers and ribbons and made stars from the wrapping paper, lying Ronnie's stocking beneath it all 'for tomorrow, from Santa'. It was going to be a great Christmas after all. Things were going to be good. Again.

Suzie's Dream

C E MARSHALL

author of Starseeker series: 'When Evil Calls', 'Wormhole', and 'Restitution'
as well as ' Quadseers', 'The Watcher', and 'Inspirational Writings'

Suzie sighed, another day at work loomed. I hope that creep Harry doesn't try to grope me again, she thought. She liked the work; it was the people that were the problem.

She opened her front door and stared out in amazement, turned round and back again. "Yes this is my house."

In front of her snow covered everything, some way away, she could see the outline of a hedge, but she lived in a town house with a short path to the road and houses all around. There was no sign of the path, the road, or any other houses, and it hadn't snowed there in decades.

She stepped into the snow and sank to the top of her shoes. She took another step and the ground vanished beneath her. She fell, and kept on falling. Around her snowflakes hid the landscape and fell with her. That's odd, I should be falling faster than the snowflakes. Suzie realised that although she was falling it felt more like gliding, which ended with a gentle bump as she landed on the ground.

Here the snow was not so deep, just a covering she realised as she got to her feet. But where was she?

"Welcome to Winterland," a voice close by called.

She looked, but could not see anyone. "Where are you?" she asked.

"Down here," the voice replied.

Suzie looked down, a tiny creature with four legs ending in splayed paws and a very human like head looked up at her hopefully.

"Come with me. I have things to show you," the creature said.

Not knowing where she was or what to do Suzie bent to pick up the creature, thinking that they would make quicker progress if she carried it.

For its size the creature moved remarkable quickly out of her reach. "No touching," it admonished. "Follow me."

So Suzie followed where it led.

The creature's paws allowed it to run swiftly over the snow, so light that it left no tracks. Suzie hurried to follow, feeling that perhaps there was a track or path beneath her. Snow still fell around her so she couldn't see far ahead. Then the ground began to rise and they entered a forest. The snow had not penetrated the canopy, but the forest floor camouflaged the creature and Suzie had to keep close. Still the ground rose until they passed out of the forest. The ground angled up and Suzie realised they were on the side of a mountain, yet, steep as the path had become she found she could climb without effort. She wasn't really dressed for this but she wasn't cold either.

At last they reached a plateau and the creature slowed. The snow stopped and the view opened up. Suzie saw her world in all its raw beauty, then suddenly it changed, and she saw the ugly thing that it had become.

Now the creature chanted:

"It's getting cold
Winter's coming.
The air is cold.
Where's my jumper, thick socks and boots?
Will it snow? Will frosts be hard?
Who can tell,
'Tis just God's will.

We'll moan and shiver if outside,
Prefer the fireside, wine in hand.
Dark evenings let loose the demons,
Hide inside, don't let them get you.
Who's hiding round the corner.
All irrational fears that come with Winter and the Darkness,
When Spring comes and light returns the fears will be forgotten.
Until then, look deep within and find the inner light and warmth
that is your spirit.

Whisper to that spirit and it will keep you safe, for it will call on
loved ones lost to higher realms and they will guard you through the
winter nights.

They calm your fears, cloak you in love, you'll be warm no matter
how cold it is outside.

With that warmth and knowledge you can calm another's fears,
turn tears to laughter, sadness into joy.

Then, when Santa comes all darkness will disperse and light fill
all your world."

"That was beautiful," Suzie said, before sadly adding, "and so
was my world as you first showed it to me. But Santa doesn't
come to me any more."

The creature looked up at her, "Gifts for children make them
happy for a while, before they are forgotten. You receive gifts all
the year, and yet you never see them."

Then the creature chanted once more:

"Frosty nights, cold windy days.

Winter is upon us.

Snow falls, each flake an individual, no two flakes alike.

Yet when they alight upon the ground they combine in
something magical.

Children come and play together, all differences forgotten.

Adults duck the snow they throw and wryly smile at memories
of times gone by,

Then continue on their way conducting the next argument within their minds.

Humans are individuals, each one different from their neighbour,

Yet so rarely when they come together do they create magic like the snow.

Dogma, hatred, jealousy all combine.

Chaos reigns.

Yet each one knows there was a time when they were carefree in the snow.

They shake their heads at memories but will not change their ways.

So it seems we're doomed to face a world in turmoil.

How simple the solution,

But none will change,

Fearing that they will be trampled by the rest.

All must change or none."

"I can't make people change," Suzie said sadly.

"But you can show them the gifts they receive and reject all through the year."

"I don't understand."

"Snow can be beautiful. Fresh rain brings delicious smells to the air. The flowers give their scent and colour. The sun warms you with its rays. Streams teem with life that few will see, waterfalls scatter the light in rainbows. Deep in jungles the animals do roam. Show them these. Maybe a few will see the beauty of these things and ask for change, maybe that change will come."

"I don't know how ... " Suzie began. But the creature and the scene were gone, as she woke up in her bed.

Who Done It?

BARB DWYER

Y'know, these elves can just feck right off. They can boot me with their pointy toes and jab me with their pointy hats all they want but they don't have the balls to follow through. Yeah, that's right! Go on, you tiny beaky Spock-eared twats! Go and jingle your bells! Jingle them all the way back to your sweet little beddy-bye-byes where you can sleep for as long as you want! Yeah, go on. Take a chance on sleeping forever, why don't ya? If it was good enough for that wee Rumplestiltskin bloke, it'll be good enough for you, ya creepy wee gobshites.

Sure, Santa's dead but he had it coming.

Jeez, I've had to listen to moan moan bleedin moans for months about him and what they were going to do about this whole mahoosive sorry mess, but do you know what? In the end they did nothing. They were too busy jabbering. They did n-o-t-h-i-n-g. De nada. Sweet Fanny Adams.

Truth is, we all watched Santa wank about for months. He'd been chuntering on about dropbox-this and wetransfer-that but we could all see that he'd lost the data way back when. The Nice and Naughty lists were l-o-n-g gone. We. Were. Fecked. Feliz Natal, my arse.

It was the moment Mrs Claus walked out that things went bits up. Every year, she'd had profiles stored from Afghanistan to Zimbabwe, all dusted and done. Done and dusted. Yep, the minute she caught the ol' man in the back of his sleigh with you-know-who, it'd all come crashing down. We. Were. Fecked. Deck the halls, my arse.

So, Santa's no more. Out of the game. Six feet under, or he will be once these elves start digging. Lazy feckers. And once they finally stop snotting and sobbing, they'll see that he was always surplus to requirements anyhoo. Sure, it's a shame that he accidentally tripped while feeding me and my mates and landed head first in a bucket of reindeer slop and somehow couldn't get himself out. Naw, it's not curious that hoof marks were found on the back of his jacket which precisely matched my front feet. I tried my level best to get him out. Proved too tricky to get the slippery ol' sucker out of a full five inches of slop.

Still, as I was saying, he was surplus to … what's that? … sure, I know the route! Clockwise round the world, of course. Stopover in Calcutta for a few carrots, a quick breather in Sydney for some mince pies and back home by sunrise. Done it every year for decades. Sure, I can shine up my red nose and get the show on the road. I'll crack on. Centre stage, this time. Where I've always belonged.

And see these elves? They can just feck right off.

Anonymous

No Name

No Way

No How

Merry Christmas!

Yo ho ho

All that

Aye, right

Thoughts

C E MARSHALL

*author of Starseeker series: 'When Evil Calls', 'Wormhole', and 'Restitution'
as well as ' Quadseers', 'The Watcher', and 'Inspirational Writings'*

Hustle and bustle, buy presents for all.

But one little baby has no presents at all.

Not even a cot that he calls his own.

No-one knows of him while they have a moan.

All have forgotten the reason for Christmas.

Know nothing of Angels and real celebration.

A king has been born, but no-one now sees.

Who goes to the stable and knocks on the door?

Who whispers soft words to Mary his mother?

Who feels the presence of angels around them?

Who understands that angels are real?

If it can't been seen, then it's not real.

Can't touch it, yet see it; only a mirage.

They want an Xbox, or perhaps a Playstation.

Or something expensive that Mum can't afford.

And never a thought for the babe we call Lord.

Natures shows wonders, and also its' fury.

No-one sees the wonder,

All quail at its fury.

When floods come along, we want someone to blame.

Blame greed and stupidity that built on flood plains.

The land it is plundered for the riches it yields.

When the riches are gone, then so are the fields.

Our world it is dying as greed bleeds it dry,

Christmas is coming, Who hears the Christ's cry?

Christmas Donkey

KATE TROUGHT

author of 'Winnie of the Dell' by Susan Trought

Onward plodding, silently

Stars, black holes

Bored, shining in the sky.

Perhaps the Father is looking through?

Onward trotting, breathlessly.

Mary more tired

Than time would allow.

Perhaps the Father will give a sign?

Onwards, onwards grey donkey

Dusty, thick-coated companion

Sure-footed

Through the night

Onwards trudging, stopping now.

Innkeeper kind

Helpless in sympathy.

Perhaps the stable would do?

Onwards sighing, shelter here.

Warm straw, sweet rosemary-

Scented hay.

Perhaps the Father is closer still?

Waiting, patient, watching

Soft eyed, dear friend

Until the Babe is born.

Christmas Punch

GINNY BRITTON

Christmas Day, 1991.

It was around 2pm when I clocked that the red wine box that sat on the window sill like an ugly tap of truth, felt rather light.

"Fill my glass, Ginny."

And like the dutiful daughter I did as I was told.

I had to tip the box to pour it and I was aware that this could work in my favour, because as the box was tipped, the clock on the wall signalled that the film I had been waiting to see was about to start. So as I handed him his glass his merriment hit happy as the Turkey was delivered from the oven.

He hauled it onto the counter top with a grunt and a heft that betrayed his unsupple joints and I got busy wrapping it in foil, then swaddling it in T towels to keep it warm while it rested. And then I picked up the TV remote. I scaled the channels and there he was, Mr River Phoenix who I was all pie eyed over alongside Harrison Ford, who these days I am also pie eyed over.... I digress though. It took his red wine fuelled brain a minute or two to realise I'd changed the channel and to begin with he ignored it but I'd noted his shift in breathing, the tightening of the corner of his mouth and an almost unseen tilt of his eyebrow, and then that pause before he carried on with what he was doing. It was a synchrony of turning potatoes, tossing the carrots in sugar and glazing the parsnips and finally finishing off the sauce with a poof of sherry. One sploosh added, one glass drunk, red wine sipped and back to warming the sauce.

Christmas sauce was a big deal in our household, it consisted of a 3-day reduction and a shed load of sherry. The rule was, buy a bottle for the sauce and a bottle for the chef and as the days passed and the reduction reduced so did the contents of bottle.

Mum was pottering in the dining room decorating the table and arranging plates and platters. I noted that she'd dressed up and had put make up on which was most unlike her. I was handed a ladle to decant the gravy into the gravy boat and the jug for the sauce was put to one side as the dinner was coming together and the turkey was now being carved.

In between slices he picked up the channel changer and switched sides but as he did so Mum said with an air of calm, "Oh, but she was watching that, won't you turn it back for her?"

What happened next is a bit of a blur. I remember a sauce pan flying; the washing up bowl hit full flight too, I can clearly see that spinning off of the woodchip walls in a confetti of bubbles.

I remember the shock. I remember me running and shoving my sister, and my little brother who was only 7 years old in a room together and telling them, "STAY HERE! JAM THAT CHAIR BEHIND THE DOOR HANDLE AND DO NOT OPEN IT UNTIL I SAY!"

I remember running back into the kitchen and seeing my dad manhandle my Mum, I do not remember how I got in between them but I do remember the punch to the side of my jaw. I remember my Mum screaming. I remember taking too long to get back up. Then I remember hearing the door slam and he was gone.

My mum dished up a dishevelled Christmas dinner like she didn't know what else to do ... her hair was all undone and her face just said everything.

I remember chewing turkey through tears and a sore jaw with my little bothers hand tightly wound around mine. He was only small and I remember him being so upset at my upset. I wonder if he remembers this now.

I remember the intolerant hurt.

Telly off ...

Mum saying with a fallen face, and a quiet voice, "Stop crying Ginny," as if the dinner was a plaster to fix what was broken.

It's very hard to eat when you are so upset.

I also remember spluttering over that dry turkey and saying I'd rather be the bird on the table. To which I was reminded that even birds have predators. To this day I cannot stomach a turkey on the Christmas table, I can still feel the threads of it around my teeth. The ball of it chewed up in my cheek, refusing to go down. So these days, on my Christmas table it's a chicken and pigs in blankets, and roasties stacked high with crackers being pulled, popping along with my children's excitement as hats are adorned and terrible jokes are giggled over. There is no anger, no fear and even the sauce has been changed over the years so that practically the only long standing ingredient is the Harvey's Bristol Cream.

I often look back on that year and how the day was in a snap second irreparably damaged along with our trust, and confidence. And I've poured all of that into ensuring that for my children, its a safe day. A lovely day and one that will be stored on the top shelf of happy memories in the catalogue of my children's childhood.

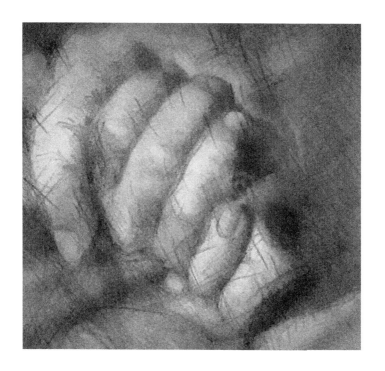

A Christmas to Remember

CAROLINE JAMES MACKIE

Christmas eh? How can it be Christmas already? It was only a few weeks ago she had found a hanging star bauble in the garden that had been hiding since last Christmas. It's also surely no more than a month or so since the boxes with the decorations got put away properly? It just can't be a year since she took them out.

Of course though, it is. Well, almost. All the adverts on the telly have been repeating for weeks already and she knows it's time to be planning some sort of menu for Christmas dinner. Always such a trauchle these days. She can't remember when it was fun. Was it ever fun? No, probably not. Not really. Ach... surely? Of course. Must not let 'events' colour the past. Of course it has often been great fun. Buck up!

There had been some memorable Christmases in the house, right enough. The one where her mother lay snoring on the couch before she'd even had her Christmas pudding - that was a howler. That one when the turkey had been so dry and disgusting it was inedible, and it transpired on top of that, that she had left the giblets, still wrapped in plastic, in the cavity too. The one when she'd known for a fact, beforehand, that the kids had found, opened and rewrapped all their presents before the day. She'd let them keep believing she didn't know, so they did all the 'oh'ing' and 'ah'ing' quite dramatically and so disingenuously, that it became even funnier. She only told them at dinner.

There was that one ... oh, it was a long time ago now, when a knock had come at the door and it had been his dad, arriving 'just in time' (late!) to surprise the kids. He was sozzled by the time he got there. How he got through the airport and all the way to them she would never know. Hilarity ensued among the kids as they rummaged in his suitcase to find the presents he'd brought them - mostly from jumble sales and 'bring and buys'. Aah, that was fun. That man!

Then there was the one, four years ago now - well, almost - when the knock at the door hadn't been quite so enjoyable. To say the least. He'd been gone ages, supposed to be getting some little messages she'd forgotten, but she'd been so busy with everyone and watching the turkey and the usual insanity with the little ones, seeing the police officers at the door really took her aback. She hadn't even had time to worry yet.

Of course the hours and the days that followed just went by in a blur really. Someone must have cleared everything away. She never did find out what happened to the turkey. The girls. They'll have done it. By the time she was actually approachable and compos mentis again, it was the day of the funeral. Weird end to that year, that's for sure. She must ask them... she'd never actually had a full account of things. All she knows really is that he was gone and she almost followed him.

Christmas was definitely cancelled that year. The year after, they'd all tried, but it was a bit subdued. By year three, last year, well, life does go on and she knew he wouldn't want her to remain unhappy forever so it had been ... well, almost normal, for Christmas. And now ... it's Christmas again.

I mean, it's not like you can forget the date, but it's supposed to be nice for kids so you can't keep being miserable. She'd have a wee bubble before they'd all arrive, that'd sort her. The place would be all pretty and decorated like they always did and they could have a lovely time and a lovely dinner and they could all do the washing up. She and the boys would play some new board game she'd get them (she's not allowed on the Play Station as she gets too het up) and they'd bring through a cuppa and a bit of

Christmas cake and some mince pies like she always used to do when the kitchen was tidied. Things would be back on track.

Next year will be a jubilee of sorts. Five is a jubilee is it not? Yes. Funny word though. Jubilee. Sounds a bit too festive for the memorial of a dead loved one. There'll be some other word more fitting, but to be fair, she wants it to be festive, and it is for Christmas. She's had an idea and will be putting it to them all on Christmas Day. She's going to take the whole Christmas abroad, somewhere warm, and everyone needs to be there, for his special remembrance. Her treat, well, her gift from this year coming up. Will take the year to arrange it all, probably, but it's happening. No dissenters, no nay-sayers. So, that's her gifts to them all sorted. No wrapping involved.

Hah, she can't wait now.

Better get digging into those boxes of decorations. Will be putting some aside to take with, next year.

Gnome Sweet Gnome

HANNAH KEMPTON

'Who is it?' he called, puzzled. Hushed voices again. They seemed to be strained, as if there was an argument going on between them.

'Who is it?' Errol called again.

'Er … postman,' the voice said gruffly.

It definitely wasn't Ern, and at seven in the evening? Doubtful. An early Christmas present?

'Who is it really?' asked Errol, suspicious.

'It's the postman,' the voice said again. 'I 'ave a… er… special delivery.'

'You don't sound like the postman,' replied Errol who was now looking around the hallway for something heavy to brandish.

'Well, what's the postman sound like?' said the voice.

Errol heard a slap and a hushed 'Ow!' from the other side of the door. He decided to continue the bizarre conversation.

'His voice isn't so crackly as yours and it's higher,' he said with a smile. Whoever this was, he obviously wasn't very bright.

'Oh,' said the voice. 'This better?' This voice was certainly a pitch higher but still sounded gravelly. Errol could still hear hushed voices, a scrabbling sound and stifled sniggers.

'No,' said Errol, with a mean grin on his face. 'You need to sound more like a girl and it still needs to go higher than that.'

There was a pause and more hushed conversation.

'I'll do it …'

' No, let Grim do it! He sounds like a girl! '

'... Hey... I do not!

'... Ow!'

'Let me in please,' said the now ridiculous high pitched voice which made the speaker cough. 'We, I mean, I need to talk to yer.'

'Why should I let you in?' asked Errol.

Another pause.

'Because I 'ave delivered summat to your 'ouse by mistake,' said the voice, which was gradually getting lower and husky with the effort of keeping up the girly squeak.

Errol remembered the rattling letterbox and looked down onto the bristle mat. There was a very dirty, folded piece of paper. He picked it up and opened it. It read:

DERE NOME,
WE NO YOU AVE IT. GIVE US IT BAK NOW.
OR ELS.
FANK YOU
P.S. YOUR GUTTER'S BROKE.

After deciphering the very bad handwriting and spelling errors, Errol screwed up the paper and threw it in the paper bin. A minute passed and Errol decided to walk away and make himself comfortable in the living room. He lit a fire in the grate and stoked up his pipe. A mellow cherry smell was released into the air and Errol sighed as he sank into his chair.

A few minutes later, he heard scuffling noises near the window. And there was the whispering again! Who the bloody hell was it and why didn't they just bugger off? Hearing footsteps in his flowerbeds was the last straw. Standing up, he marched over to the front door, grasped the handle and was about to twist, when another note landed on the mat. Again, it was grubby and contained the same scrawled handwriting and bad grammar.

DERE NOME,

WE R CONDUKTIN A SURVAY ROUND ERE AND NEED TO COM IN TO CONDUK THE SURVAY WHAT WE IS CONDUKTIN.

FANK YOU

'Bloody burglars, that's what they are. Trying to get me to invite them in! The cheek,' thought Errol. With a newfound anger, he twisted the handle on the front door and opened it, ready to tell the culprits quite what they could do with their notes and silly surveys.

No one.

Closing his mouth, the rant left unranted, Errol looked around the garden and found nothing except a trampled flowerbed to match his ruined lawn. Frowning at nothing in particular, he turned away from the door and mentally composed a speech of threats and swearwords that he would aim at the cheeky beggars if he got his hands on them.

Suddenly, a pair of running feet got louder and louder and as Errol turned around, they were leaping through his front door and onto his polished wooden floorboards. The feet slipped and slid, trying to gain purchase, and only stopped when they connected painfully with the staircase and then lay twitching in a heap on the floor. The feet were connected to a short, dirty looking thing with large ears, a wide mouth and speckled, greasy looking green skin. It had skinny limbs but a protruding, fat belly, long spindly fingers and a squashed and wrinkled head. The smell was pungent and musty, like a damp towel mixed with stale manure. A belch came from the crumpled mess and then a groan of effort as it eased itself into a sitting position. It gave a sniff, which turned into a full-blown snort inward, resulting in a rough, ill sounding cough complete with phlegm. The thing wiped its mouth on the back of its arm, leaving a snotty brown trail. This was then wiped on its ragged tunic making this deposit the most recent of stains. The stains of many colours would have made for a bright and attractive garment, had the colours not have originated from various orifices of the yet unnamed atrocity currently sitting in Errol's hallway.

Errol could do nothing but stare as the intruder gradually composed itself enough to make eye contact. It blinked and shook its head before picking its nose and adding the results of its search to the tunic, adding texture as well as colour, before shakily heaving itself up onto unsteady feet and swaying a bit before grabbing the banister for support. At this point, two other similar looking beings stumbled through the door, panting for breath and pointing angrily at the still wobbly guest who was now rubbing its head and wincing. There was, Errol now noticed, a slimy brownish green 'splat' at the foot of the stairs where the thing had collided so heavily with the bottom step. Grimacing, he tried to think of what potion he had under the sink that would remove it completely.

It's funny how one thinks of the most mundane, everyday things when one is surrounded by strange, unknown beings in one's home.

A Merry E-Christmas!

LEA TAYLOR

author of 'The House Beside the Cherry Tree'
'Midlothian Folk Tales', and 'Animals Beasties and Monsters of Scotland'

Normally all in the household would have been in a state of frantic activity, particularly in the stable with the reindeer, but this year it was different. This year it was quiet and all the reindeer looked down in the mouth.

"Why so glum?" asked one of the elves as he filled the stalls with straw.

"Well how would you feel if you were being replaced?" ventured Rudolf

"Replaced?" the elf spun round in his green tights and adjusted his hat that had fallen over his face.

"Bloody COP" muttered Rudolf, pawing the ground with his hoof.

"Climate crisis ... what about reindeer crisis?" guerned another reindeer.

"Centuries of service and next thing you know they're installing a pod on the front of the house and just like that the sleigh becomes electric, and we're out of a job." The reindeer lowered his head and a single tear ran down his cheek.

"Oh dear! Oh dear oh dear!" said the elf and ran to the kitchen.

Ms Claus (she wasn't married) put the tray of mince pies down, wiped her floury hands and listened closely.

"Oh dear," she said, "Oh dear oh dear!"

She went to Santa who was busy pouring over world maps and lists of names and whispered in his ear. He tugged on his white beard and with knitted eyebrows said. "Oh dear, oh dear oh dear."

He took off his glasses, donned his hat and coat and went out to the stable.

"Come reindeers, gather round," he said, extending his arms wide.

They pricked their ears, eyes bright and stood close, hoof to hoof, antler to antler listening in to what Santa had to say.

"There is to be no electric sleigh, and certainly no replacement of reindeers. Its business as usual, so forget all this nonsense!"

"But …" ventured the smallest of reindeer, "what about climate change won't we be adding to it with our methene?"

Santa chuckled and ruffled the reindeer's ears, "No, not at all, I feed you with sustainable food that stops the worst of the farting, havent you noticed?"

The reindeer stopped, looked at his rear end and sniffed. "Ohh, I have rather lost my pong!"

The rest tittered, showing reindeer teeth behind rubbery, whiskered lips.

"And besides," said Santa, "I'd never get an electric sleigh around the world. It wouldn't have nearly enough range."

"It's called *range-anxiety*," said Rudolf rising up tall on his forehooves feeling quite important and knowledgeable.

"Now, enough of this silly nonsense and start getting yourselves ready for the big event. Alright?"

The reindeer shuffled sheepishly.

"Alright?" Santa repeated.

"Yes!" they chorused.

"Right then, must be off." And with that Santa vanished in a sprinkle of fairy dust.

No sooner had the door closed when all the reindeer began cheering, kicking the doors with their hooves and singing in unison "… dashing through the snow, without an electric sleigh, merrily we go, laughing all the way …"

The Day We Traded Gratitude For Entitlement

HELEN MONAGHAN

author of 'The Magical Mix of Money of Tax', 'Successful Business Minds', and '12 Steps to Improve Your Cashflow'

Once upon a time, Christmas was an occasion where we celebrated a miracle, or at least so the legend goes. As Suzi sipped her coffee she couldn't help wondering if the story had been distorted over time. What if the big deal wasn't the virgin birth at all, or even Jesus himself, but the birth alone? This certainly made her feel better and frankly, she'd take whatever she could this morning.

When John sat down beside her on the sofa she figured she'd get his input. "Do you think we've got the Christmas story all wrong?"

"Eh?"

"You know, Jesus, the virgin birth and all that?"

"I never had you down as the religious type."

"I'm not, just thinking."

John sighed and glanced in the direction of the bathroom, "Is this what I think it's about?"

Suzi lowered her head into her mug. "We'll get pregnant one day. It's just not the right time for us." He reached across and enveloped her into a hug.

"How do you know for sure?" she muffled into his chest.

John blew out the tension he'd been holding on to for the last hour.

"To be honest I don't, but we can always adopt if it doesn't. Plus, I sometimes think having kids is overrated anyway. I'm tired of James moaning about how crap his life is now he's a Dad."

"Some people just don't know how lucky they are!" Suzi jumped from his embrace.

"Couldn't agree more."

"Would you think that too?" she cautiously enquired.

"No. It's just everyone has this fantasy about how awesome their life will be after having kids but nothing changes. Well, apart from the obvious but they're still at the same job, still live in the same town, have the same friends, still married to the same person ... I'm just saying what we already have is fabulous. We're both happy with everything, well apart from this but ... so instead of getting down about a negative result let's focus on all the positive stuff going on."

"Like be grateful for everything?"

"Yeah, I mean we have a lot to be grateful for. We both have good jobs, money in the bank, a fabulous home, some half-decent friends, and touch wood, our health is pretty alright too."

"You're right you know. I stumbled on a book last summer when the pandemic was getting to me that suggested we ought to be grateful for our lives. The guy, I've forgotten his name now, but he was a church minister and he was talking more in the context of death I think, but what I took from it was that we've lost the idea of what life actually is."

"Which is?"

"Well, we only have to look at a human biology book to see just how complex we really are. It's a wonder we're even alive at all! It's like humanity decided to replace gratitude with entitlement once upon another time."

"Yeah, totally agree. When I was studying psychology, we touched on neuroscience. I read about a guy who couldn't pick anything up, some malfunction between the nerves in his hand and his brain or something. I spent the entire day saying thanks to my hands every time I picked up my cup of tea or my pen!"

"What did that feel like it?"

"To hold a pen?" John laughed, "No silly."

Suzi slapped him on the arm. "What I mean is, how did it feel to be grateful all day long, for something we deem such a basic thing? I've tried it but I'm lucky if I get to lunchtime!"

"Oh, it was amazing! I felt at ease with everything. I had an assignment due the next day but I wasn't freaking out at all. The words just flowed out of me and I got my first, and last, A."

"Wow. So this church minister, and all the others, are on to something then? Gratitude is the key to life. It's where the magic happens."

"Absolutely, or at least I think so. The same happened when I met you. I was so grateful you said yes to meeting up again, so much so when I was made redundant the next day, I was totally unfazed by it all. As it turns out it was the best thing that happened to me. Well, that and you."

Suzi snuggled into him, savouring the rare romantic moment. She knew he was overdoing it, desperately trying to make her feel better but she was grateful nonetheless. "So do you think we've got life wrong then? I mean some of the news feeds really irked me last year. Like the one where we had to make sure we didn't let our loved ones die before their time. I totally understand what it was asking us to do, and I respected that, but it also implied that we're entitled to old age. Like, if we die before we're ninety-odd, it's due to the negligent actions of others, or as a result of a mistake, we've made. The same goes for births too. If we can't get pregnant, we must be doing something wrong!"

"Aye, it would appear that way…"

"Also did you know that there are almost three thousand stillbirths every year? No one talks about that."

"Yikes... You know I reckon life is a puzzle that gets thrown up in the air and what happens next very much depends on how it all lands. If one tiny microscopic piece is missing or finds itself upside down, or in the wrong place, the whole thing collapses. Sometimes someone beats the odds, which then brings it back to luck I guess. You know it really freaks me out that I'm now older than my Dad ever was. Life really is a gift. Old age too."

"And I reckon if we look hard enough, we can see the pandemic is nudging to wake us up to the miracle of life itself."

Mimi's Xmas Story

MIMI SERTHELON (AGED 7)

One Xmas Eve a little boy called Tim, without asking, opened all his presents.

His first one was a car, his second was a Furby. It looked evilly into his eyes but Tim did not care and went on to his next present - but every time Tim looked away the Furby took another step forward. When he looked back he was confused, then he said, "Did my Furby just move? Oh well." He shrugged and went to his third present.

Three minutes later when he was opening his last present his Mum came downstairs and said, "How dare you open your presents without asking me?" Tim knew he was in big trouble but he couldn't help it. "So you only want coal for next Xmas then?" said Mum.

"Nooooo" said Tim.

When it was bed time time he said good night to his Furby and went to sleep. When Tim woke up in the morning his Furby was gone. He called to his Mum for breakfast but she didn't reply so he went to look for her. She wasn't there.

Tim was very scared but he knew it must be a dream. So he went to his mum's room and noticed that her shoes weren't there. Tim then went to check to see if her wallet was on the kitchen counter but instead he found his Furby on the floor, eating bread.

"Who are you?" shouted Tim but the Furby just winked.

Tim ran away.

The Furby moved slowly after him.

Tim went outside and the Furby did not move an inch when it got to the front door. Tim laughed. It was allergic to the sunlight.

The Furby turned red because It was angry.

"I hate you. I done a crime so your Mum got sent to prison," said the Furby as he laughed back.

"Why are you angry at me?" asked Tim.

"I just want to be with my family" It cried.

"Well I ca ..." but before Tim could say his final words, the Furby jumped at him but this caused It to get a rash from the sun. It lay on the ground and closed it's eyes which turned red.

Tim could see the Mum-Furby rushing to get her baby but Tim's mum came and slapped Mum-Furby with her handbag.

"You're a monster," Tim's Mum shouted.

"No," Tim said angrily.

The baby Furby jumped up and ran to it's Mum.

"Let's leave them," shrugged Tim, "I hope I don't have a Christmas like that again."

The End.

Santa's Full Sack

DANIEL DUGGAN

Ahh, there's my dad, asleep on the landing, Santa hat on his head, ho ho holy night snoring. He must have been downstairs putting the presents under the tree. They were always in black bin bags. We would pick a gift and unwrap straight back into the rubbish sack. Saved time when tidying up. He must have noshed down the two mince pies meant for the reindeer before he knocked back that double measure of whisky left for Father Christmas. Being Santa, and our house being his last stop, that final drink must have tipped him over the edge. He nearly made it to bed, but that one night's work must have caught him before he could lay his head on the pillow. I step over him and go to the kitchen to put the kettle on. By the time I've made a strong pot of tea, dad's sitting up in bed next to mum. The elves must have woken him. I don't say a word, tinsel threading my lips shut.

There But For The Grace of God

BETSY ANDERSON

Once upon a time in a world far far away
Morning was breaking, heralding the day
The tree adorned with jewels and lights
Sparkled to reveal a bounty of delights
The thunder of feet stampeding down the stairs
Squeals of excitement, bouncing like hares
The warm scent of Christmas filled the air
Gathering families together from everywhere
Weeks of planning, preparation and worry
Gone in a frenzied present opening flurry
At the same time, in a world right here
Men, women and children are living in fear
Cold, hungry, tired and weak

Their circumstances are desperate, bleak

Washed up on shores, fleeing pain

Nothing to lose and much to gain

Christmas for them, a different sense of arrival

Fighting for their very survival

Delight in the joy that Christmas brings

Raise a glass, laugh till your heart sings

But take a moment, with a respectful nod

Recognise … there but for the Grace of God

The Greatest Gift

ANNIE MCDONNELL

My StepMom, Carmela was like a Christmas present dipped in fancy Easter egg colors with a huge magnificent bow and 4th of July sparklers attached. The kind of gift you get and don't want to open because it's just so perfect.

Carmela was always a holiday celebration because every day was a holiday to her. She enjoyed life. She was a gift of hope, love and laughter, but mostly security and faith.

Each of her hugs embraced my soul and lifted me up high. I can still feel her in the soft, warm breeze that caresses my face every once in a while. It arrives when I need her most.

I cried in her lap a month before she died & asked what I would do without her. She said "you love the moon, it's always there watching over you. If you need me, that's where I'll be"! She was dying still comforting me, as a mother would.

My StepMom was like an island I could swim far away from yet return to as often as I wanted to, especially if I needed rest or care.

Our love existed because of the trust we gave to each other with our whole hearts. It flourished because I felt like I was part of her. I felt like I was always hers. It survives still because she hasn't left me.

My StepMom brought out my joy when I thought it had been lost forever. She reminded me that I was loved more than those 1000 cuts and scars that were trying to take my soul, For most of my life she was one of my truest of loves because she knew me most and still loved me.

My StepMom always understood me. She understood my losses, fears and traumas. She even understood my weaknesses and faults and loved me in spite of them. She loved me even if I made mistakes. Her eyes saw only the best in me and forgave me when necessary.

Isn't this exactly how you should feel about your mother? Feeling wrapped in their love and security like a warm winter scarf on the coldest of days.

My StepMom had stunning strength and will-power. When I was burdened or struggling or felt alone she was there for me. I trust her love and support is traveling across the heavens to me.

When she needed me, caring for her was the least I could do. It was definitely the most Beautiful and honorable responsibility I have ever had. I become her fierce, loyal and mama bear protector for nine months. Now I realize it was simply her love looking back at me because I was only returning all the love she had ever given me.

I remember getting her to the bathroom was difficult so I'd pretend we were dancing all the way there. I would sing, and she would always laugh. We were happy.

I tried to make her dying as special as she made my life. She thanked me a few times me saying I made dying fun. That's a special conversation that I loved.

I wasn't sure who I'd be without her. I still wonder.

It's very difficult when Mother's Day arrives. I always needed her love that day because she was the only person that recognized me as a Mom, too, since miscarrying my baby girl, Savannah Alexis at 5 months.

She was my biggest champion. If I had even the slightest cold she would be at my doorstep with homemade chicken noodle soup, magazines and a coloring book. When I was diagnosed with RA, she got me a bag full of goodies for my infusion days full of more books and a day planner to keep my appointments together.

I keep the copy of a card she wrote to a coworker of mine on the refrigerator to remind me how much I had been loved by her. He shared it with me while I was grieving her. I was grieving so hard I still wasn't able to breathe, he believed this would bring me comfort and it did. My StepMom had asked him to watch over me when she was gone because "I do so much for others and deserve it. She said she knew I'd be lonely and in need of love without her. She asked Angelo to love me and make sure I was surrounded by love. Carmela once told me I needed love like people needed air, I was desperately seeking it all the time. She is right.

My stepmom was dying and thinking of me again. I believe she is now living in the heart beat of my friends.

To be loved by Carmela was warm and encouraging. Never boastful or loud. Never petty or competitive. Her love was never divided.

I hope everyone has this love in their life. We all deserve a Carmela. My gratitude is immense.

God granted me her fierce love, support, devotion and mama bear protection for almost 20 years.

My StepMom, Carmela is what unconditional love is and I am so grateful to know exactly what that feels like.

Unconditional Love. The greatest gift of all. It's everything.

I love and miss you, Mom.

Love, your Cinderella. (My nickname as she jokingly said she was the wicked StepMother.)

Mrs Claus

KAISHA JAYNE

Multi award winning blogger

Bows - check.

Tags - check.

Sellotape - double check.

Mentally praise self for remembering to buy sellotape - check.

Gift bags - check.

Presents.....AH CRAP! I thought I was doing exceptionally well then! I mean, I did remember to buy sellotape, that alone should be grounds for an award nomination. Of course I would need actual presents for the sellotape to become a useful investment. Nobody in their right mind would brave the busy, Edinburgh streets in November, purposely to buy Christmas presents for all 256433547585 (SLIGHT exaggeration) members of your family, only to come home with zilch presents. Nothing. Not even the yearly, on sale gift (anything less than 70% would be daylight robbery) which has no set recipient, yet always gets given out eventually as the 'emergency gift'. Nada. Zilch. Absolutely sweet f'all. Well, except for everything pretty to wrap the imaginary gifts in - I nailed that! If only my sister was into Harry Potter - I could EASILY wrap up air and pretend it's come from the not-so-hidden realm of 'under the stairs'. She's that gullible.

'Ringgggggggggg, ringgggggg'. The sound of my mobile phone brings me back down to Earth. It's 3pm on a Saturday afternoon and, whilst I know my best friend, Issy, is still at work in the local toy shop, part of me (no, A LOT of me) wishes that her name will be flashing on my phone right about now. But, just to make my mood even more festive, ahem, I peak at the screen with one eye open and see that it is indeed Mrs Claus herself. My mother. No, I'm not even joking. My surname is Claus. My mother is married to Stephen Claus, therefore she is indeed, Mrs Claus.

"Mother! What do I owe this pleasure on a Saturday afternoon? Finished visiting the elves already?" My mother groans down the phone so loudly that if I didn't know any better, I would have thought she released gasses whilst inhaling helium.

"Holly, please don't be so facetious. It's November for goodness sake, I do not go and visit the 'elves' as you so eloquently put it, until December. Do keep up girl!"

Oh and I'M the one being facetious? "Well they're children, they're the same size as elves though aren't they?"

I have nothing against children, obviously, I just think that they resemble elves in height. Plus, being 4ft 10 with a name like 'Holly Claus', I don't fancy being an elf on my own this Christmas. Again.

"Oh darling, no! You're the only elf that I know!" (See, what did I tell you.) Mrs Claus continues to bend my ear; "I was only calling you to see how you were getting on with your Christmas shopping. Ivy called me earlier to say she had bought everything on her list. Although I'm not really surprised! If you're not sorted soon I don't know WHAT you'll do! There are only 51 days until Christmas day you know, Holly!"

"Er...er..that's great mum. Erm, can I call you later? I'm just about to pay for ALL of my Christmas presents and I don't like to be rude. BYE!!!" I don't even give my mum a chance to say goodbye as I just know she would question my shopping for two reasons:

1) She knows fine well that I wouldn't have bought every single one of my Christmas presents in one day.
2) Refer to point one.

I'm not surprised that my sister, Ivy, has managed to buy all of her Christmas presents as she works most of December! Oh, and yes, my parents did do THAT if you hadn't already noticed; twin daughters, a surname of 'Claus', let's just name our children 'Holly' and 'Ivy'. They won't get bullied, nooooo, not at all. Unfortunately, we did. But, at least I can say that my name represents my personality to a T; prickly!

If Mrs Claus is in this mood already with 51 days left to go, I am dreading Christmas even more than I thought. Thank goodness for mince pies!

Our Christmas Tradition

SOPHIE DEVEREUX

It's the 23rd of December
Christmas is nearly here
Whilst everyone is filled with excitement
And doing last minute shopping
I stand here in the darkness staring at the cast iron gate
Those familiar feelings looming above me like ravenous vultures
Guilt, Love, Shame
I've left it too long between visits as usual
I know I promise every year it will be different.

The children rush to find your headstone,
each desperate to be the first to say
"Hi Uncle Happy Birthday!!
They slip effortlessly into chatting about their latest news
Whilst I drag my feet far behind them
Trying to create an image of you in my mind
To chatter aimlessly to as I kneel by your graveside
And arrange the flowers the girls chose
I chide myself for only doing this once a year
Heartbroken in the knowledge that for the other 364 days a year
Your earth bed seems dreary, abandoned and unloved

I catch you up with my own developments in my life

Secretly hoping that you already know it all from watching over
me

My mind wanders, imagining who you would have been
Would you have been the kind of brother who always picked me
up with big open arms
Every time my world crumbled
Would you have been a positive role model for your nieces or a
bad influences teaching them all the things they shouldn't know
Would you have been more like Mum or Dad
Would you have been proud of me and the choices I've made
I could create a infinite lifetimes with different versions of you
And get lost in pretending that you are here

The icy wind brings me back to my stark reality
I always forget how cold it gets here and how quickly the
daylight fades
Just like that it's time to go, over far too soon
Our Christmas tradition
One that nobody would wish for
But it's woven into our history as concretely as gazing at the
night sky hoping to see a sleigh
Or waking up at the crack of dawn rummaging through our
stockings trying to guess what wonders lie inside

As I relieve a flower from your arrangement
A bit of you to keep with me however briefly
"I'll see you soon big brother," I whisper
We both know I lie
Because every time I have leave you behind and return to the
warmth of my car
It feels like I'm losing the idea of you all over again.

Serenity

MARY McCARTHY

Peace on earth and goodwill to all men.

The earworm crawls round and round in her brain. And what happens if you can't handle the peace? What happens if you need your pain, rely on it? Ask your sponsor. She'll know.

The iron dump dumps on the board. School uniforms colluding in the lie. Trying not to look around the room, into the other rooms. Great plans made during drunken hazes. Daily drunken dazes. Dump. Hiss.

"Yes, let's rip up the carpets tonight; we'll get new ones next week. We'll finish the plastering, sort out the kitchen, buy new furniture and have a holiday in the sun."

Dump.

"The interest rate on those loans isn't as bad as it seems. Just remember that's the daily rate – the annual rate is much closer to being reasonable. I can easily afford the repayments."

Dump. Hiss.

Anyway, there are still a few weeks left before Christmas. Plans made when drunk are frighteningly real when sober. Get the living room ready. Put up the tree that will provide all the light and hope that we need. All's well when the tree is up. Set the traps for the mice in the bedrooms. Clear enough space in the kitchen to prepare the feast. Clear the rotting food out of the fridge to make space for the preparations. New Year's dinner is her turn this year. New Year: new hopes, new dreams, new beginnings. Well, it can't be any worse than last year.

Kids will be home soon. A few hours and they'll be in bed. Then all will be well. That wee individual glass bottle of wine is nestling amongst the underwear in her drawer, through in the room. Three months sober. It was all just an exaggeration, you know. Storm in a teacup. She gave up to keep everyone happy. Went to AA to keep them off her back. But three months proves it. That wee bottle, singing to her from the bedroom, "Drink me …" So, no hangover this morning, then. She knew she was right.

Leave it a few days and then try two large glasses. Here's the plan: buy a whole bottle this time, drink two glasses and then put it away. Go back in a couple of days and have two more. Then there'll be a wee drop left to make a decision about.

It's amazing how much you can get through when you feel motivated! Get stuck in about the cleaning in the house, music blasting to herald the good news: she's not really an alky and can have just a wee drink to take the edge off. Relieve some of the pressure. Hope for the future.

"You're in a good mood, mum. Have you had a good day?"

"Yes, brilliant day. I might even think about going back to work soon!"

"That's amazing. Well done. Listen, we were thinking. Why don't we have dinner at dad's this New Year? You could still cook – you know you're the best – but his house is more … set up for visitors."

"I'll manage it. You know what I'm like when I get going. It will all be done – just watch me. I've had a great day, great week."

"Well, let's just keep that in reserve then. You're doing great, really!"

How is anyone ever going to be able to get better when no-one has any faith in them? A bad few months and everyone forgets who you are, what you can do, what you can achieve. If they supported her more, she wouldn't need to feel like this.

As if she wouldn't be ready for Christmas. Look at all the Christmases she managed to deliver before this wee hurdle, all the New Year dinners and parties. Well, she would show them. Maybe not wait for a few days to get that bottle. After the disappointment of being let down, the sheer disloyalty, anyone would need a glass of wine to get through. Just the two glasses, mind. There was no hangover after one but she didn't know about two. Might be a wee bit groggy tomorrow, the tolerance will have decreased. Three months is like resetting the clock – an alcohol virgin.

"Mum, where are you going, at this time of night? It's dark and freezing outside."

"We don't have enough milk for tomorrow's breakfast, sweetheart. I'm just nipping down to the Spar to get some. I'm going to walk – the fresh air will do me good."

"I'll come with you."

"No, no. No point in both of us getting cold. I'll bring you back some sweets."

"Please let me come with you. Please."

"No, I insist. I won't be long. Stay here, in the warm."

Three minutes to ten. God, she's good at this. That first bottle must have been lower alcohol. This one will be better. Just one more glass, though. Not going to overdo it. Sneak in with the sweets, say goodnight and take it to bed. No harm done. Tomorrow, we'll get the tree down from the loft. Hello, my friends, hello. She couldn't say she had missed them but they were, at least, familiar. Ghosts of Christmas past, lurking and winking in the shadows. Christmas present – no, she wasn't ready to say hello to him. If they had just supported her more, she would have made it, been ready, got everything done. Anyone would have had to drink if they had to put up with what she had to put up with. It wasn't her fault.

"Mum, why are you sitting in the dark? Where is the dinner? Have you cooked it?"

"No, sorry. I've not been feeling very well today. Here, let me phone for a takeaway. I'll pay. I won't come to your dad's – you all enjoy your dinner without me. I'll be fine."

Of course, she would be fine. She had her ghosts, her pain and her best friend for company.

Another Covid Christmas

MAGDALENA HOLLINGSBEE

Christmas card rhyme/carol to the tune of "Holly Jolly Christmas"

Well it's another Covid Christmas –
Keep your masks a'near.
Be sure to sanitise your hands
And keep viral-free your cheer.

Reflect upon the losses,
Be glad that you're still here,
Meet and greet still-distanced,
And hold tight those you hold dear.

Learn lessons from the lockdowns
By minimising fear
And forget unimportant nonsense ...
It's been another challenged year.

For presents just give presence
If cashflow's a little queer
And honour each and every moment …
Who knows what will next app?

A Covid Christmas is a time
When gratitude must be sincere.
For what remains is always love
Whatever else has disappeared.

The Snowman

MAY HALYBURTON

author of 'Around the World with Bessy - Part One – Europe',
'Around the World with Bessy - Part One and a Half - Bessy Goes Busking',
and 'Around the World with Bessy - Part Two - New York'

Jack gulped down the thick, cold night air. The familiar scent of home filled his entire being and nostalgia had begun to thaw the edges of his chilled heart. Anxiously, he scrutinised every inch of Ivy Square, imprinting the scene in his memory, terrified he should forget even the smallest detail. He had missed this place so much. This was home.

"If only I could stay here forever," he wished silently. He knew that was impossible though and so scolded himself for wasting precious moments and immediately reminded himself how lucky he was to be able to return here for a few days each year.

Standing tall in the Remembrance Rose garden, Jack turned his attention to the neat rows of cottages that protectively hugged the four sides of the square. Each roof was trimmed with sparkling, silver lights that deftly wound their way down into the gardens below, spiralling round trees and fences and anything else that crossed their glittering path. Candles quivered in the windows, their reflections nervously flickering in Jack's dark shiny eyes as his gaze passed over them, before finally settling on the holly wreath that hung slightly off centre on the bright berry-red door of number 17. So many memories were behind that door. So many memories.

Jack shivered and pulled his scarf tighter round his neck. The soft, green wool was becoming threadbare in places but he wore it with pride as if it were an Olympic medal. Christina had given it to him the very first time they met on that snowy Christmas Eve all those years ago and he had adorned it every year since, without fail.

Ivy Square was beautiful all year round, but it had a special magic at Christmas time. The huge Christmas tree sported thousands of tiny silver lights and became the meeting place for all the residents. Beside it, a small ice rink, encased in a white picket fence, buzzed with activity late into the night, as families held hands and skated round with varying degrees of ease. Wooden stalls like miniature cabins housed hand crafted gifts for sale and others served hot chocolate, doughnuts, mulled wine and mince pies.

Jack had looked on silently, as the festive activity ebbed and flowed over the holidays. He always felt included even though he was a mere spectator. However, a warmth crept over him and he knew it would soon be time to leave. Reluctantly, he bowed his head and gave in to the deep sleep that engulfed his pale shrinking body.

The berry-red door of number 17 slowly opened and Christina shuffled gingerly down the slushy path and crossed the road into the Remembrance Rose garden. She paused to take a breath, then slowly bent down as far as her aged body would allow, one hand shakily clinging on to her walking stick, the other, reaching for an old green tatty scarf that was lying in a puddle of slush and mud. Clutching the soggy garment tightly in her spindly, misshaped fingers, an expression full of love enveloped her wizened face.

"Goodnight Jack," she sighed, her watery eyes searching the starry night sky. "Until next year ..."

First Time With Snow

LIAM PATERSON

I was born in the spring, tiny and blind.

I grew through the months to become a tabby of my kind.

Food, cuddles and sleeping are all very well, but that place outside the door is where the interesting stuff dwells.

So, friendly human can I leave home? I've seen it through the window and I feel the urge to roam.

Come on, I'll be fine, I've got all the skills. And there's things out there that I'd quite like to kill.

What? Er, I meant make some friends so please beg my pardon. I've seen others like me coming into my garden.

They need a few lessons in manners I suppose and I'm just the girl to give them a slash on the nose.

What? No, I mean I'll be perfectly nice. Though maybe not to those birds or them mice.

OK, I promise I won't take a bite but please let me out or I'll make noise all night.

And ... yes the human is opening the door. They say something about snowing but I don't care no more.

I can't wait to get out and act big and tough so I leap from the door into ... what is this stuff?

It's white and cold and sticks to my fur. Ruins all my plans to give the garden a whirl.

It makes my paws wet and there's no sort of scent. Where has my lovely garden went?

I give this snow stuff a hiss. For now I think I will give the outdoors a miss. Until the weather changes and then watch out! There's gonna be hell when I'm prowling about!

Snowdrift Wreath

DANIEL DUGGAN

My hair is wintering,
a snowdrift wreath
with ginger clusters
that are fingertip clinging,
like the last
of the autumn leaves.

I tongue the rafters
of my barn door mouth,
whilst draped across my lips
is a tree knot,
a hiding spot.
A burl of words forgot.

What remains on my breath
is a waxen effigy scratched from embers,
a kist, jam packed with held tongues.

I didn't speak

and the trees fell

I didn't speak

and now there are no nests

for the returning birds.

I didn't speak,

I just let the rainbow rust.

Cat in the Cradle

BRONWEN JOHN

author of 'Crooked: Honest Criminality'

It's the sign of womanhood, Michael inwardly thinks, the first high heels on the bottom stair. Little shit, he grumbles internally as he kicks them out of harms reach to avoid a fall.

It is the annual Christmas tree lighting in Denver and all the family are going. He's leaving later then meeting his ATF team there. His wife has left with their other sons. That leaves the middle two. The niece and Calean – dawdling as usual.

They've spent their lives dawdling, bar both being born prematurely, usually straight into mischief which leaves him apologising.

He winces at the onslaught of memories.

His niece is fiddling with her shortened brown hair, laughing at a joke that her slightly younger cousin has told. She's trying to put a sprig of holly in it, but it slides out as it always has of her fine hair. She is now beyond hope with her giggling and then tuneless humming of what Mike believes to be the Welsh hymn 'Ar hyd y nos.' She glances over and flashes a happy smile, waving at him.

It takes him back to when she was little, holding onto his pant leg and big brown eyes gazing adoringly upwards and hanging onto his every word. Where were those days?

He hopes those days aren't gone.

The only reason she's in Denver for Christmas is to prevent her hearing the poison from her paternal family in the wake of her fathers death.

Everything he knows from experience with his niece knows she doesn't really show hurt; it comes out in a cacophony of writing louder than any scream she could achieve. Now he knows he's seeing the actress, lulling people into a false security when she's really writing like a demon.

She's screaming at the world but remaining miserably silent. She's already learned the three-word lie, "I am fine," to anyone's query how she is. She's an adult at sixteen when she was merely a teenager at fifteen a few weeks before. A woman.

Mind, despite womanhood, she still has ink-soaked messy hands. She still steals his battered fedora and leather jacket. Still fall asleep on his shoulder, him arm around her while watching movies. Now though she wakes and gives him a dirty look.

"We're on our way, Mike," she still bursts in, but pauses when she sees him looking at her. "What's wrong? Oh, and Caelan's asking can we borrow the car?"

"Sure thing, just thinking of an old song," he says, humming the old Harry Chapin song.

She looks at him inquisitively before she steps over goes on tiptoes to kiss his cheek. "I'll never cat and cradle you," she promises firmly.

"You're my second dad, Mike. Better than Dad."

Michael watches the two head off blasting Christmas carols. She's left red lipstick on his cheek and she's made him cry.

Still the same little shit.

Who is Santa Claus?

ROSS HARTSHORN

author of 'All Square' and 'Life is Not a Rehearsal'

5.30pm Christmas Eve 1984. It is a very dark, dismal and dank evening, the drizzling rain far removed from the deep, crisp and even snow one would like to expect at this festive time of year.

I am delivering a last, desperate Christmas card, probably in response to a greeting arriving unexpectedly late from someone I had completely forgotten about. Scarily, my postman duties have taken me to one of the less salubrious districts in my suburban new town and my visit is expected to be a quick one, largely to ensure the safety of my car.

Like a vision and completely without warning, there appears from the misty gloom an apparition clothed in a hooded red suit. On closer inspection the figure has a fluffy white beard complimented by straggly white hair protruding from the red hood, itself festooned with a brilliant white, jingling bobble. To complete the picture, this being has a sack of packages on his back and is riding a bicycle.

In that instant I am reduced to a bewildered, stunned and jabbering wreck. I watch in wonder as this eerie spirit dismounts from his bicycle and proceeds to visit each house in the terrace lining this street. As his knock on each door is answered, excited children and incredulous parents permeate the air with unbridled joy and wonderment as the apparition hands out small packets of sweets and wishes everyone a very merry Christmas.

Could this really be Santa Claus? Is my sanity truly being tested to its limits?

As he reaches the last one in the row of houses, I move closer and closer to this mistic gentleman, until I am within touching distance of him.

He is a younger end teenager with, oh, such a brilliantly happy and serene demeanour. To my absolute astonishment I recognise him as one of the members of the youth club I have spent time volunteering with. I know immediately that he is from a family of six children, all under the age of fifteen. He is the eldest. This is a family that would not be out of place in a Charles Dickens' novel, definitely living in poverty by today's standards. They survived on very little.

When I ask the lad about these Christmas Eve exploits, he compellingly explains to me that he sincerely believes in the magic of Santa Claus and, for reasons he cannot put into words, always has held in his heart the gratifying desire to make people happy at Christmas. This is his special time. He loves it so much that he started his annual gift run when he was 12 years old and will continue it into the future.

What a simple and wonderful philosophy. Without doubt, this charming boy Santa Claus is the embodiment of the Christmas spirit, spirit being the operative word. Santa Claus somehow makes tangible all that is good in humanity: peace, love and goodness.

Santa Claus is in fact in all of us, each and every one. We are all Santa Claus. Santa Claus is a state of mind.

That evening had a profound and inspiring effect on my whole outlook on life, mostly at Christmas, but in a wider sphere also. For sure, Christmas has become extra special for me. It is great to try to make Christmas magical for as many people as possible, be it through Christmas lights, Christmas jumpers, tiny gifts or singing carols. The Santa Claus latent in everyone sometimes struggles to get out. Don't be too shy or too reserved to let the spirit of Christmas take you over, even for just a short time – you will love the feeling.

P.S.   Oh, that boy? 2 years ago, 35 years after that truly amazing and life changing event, I bumped into him while out shopping, each of us recognising the other instantly. He is now married with grown up children. I entrusted him with the fact that his actions that night had been a life changing inspiration to me.

"Oh, my Santa Claus excursion," he said, "I still do that every year."

The Ladies of Six

LIAM McKNIGHT

author of 'Bob Dylan Stole My Banana'

Where I was born, almost so long ago that I wouldn't care to number it, I grew up in country much like this. I wasn't a farm boy but most all of my friends were.

The farms they lived on grew grapes for wine, sometimes even picking them in the earliest days of winter when they were frozen to make wines that tasted so sweet that even honey seemed tart by comparison. The arable farmers grew beets, peas, cabbages and sprouts, those fields smelled fetid like a promise of broken wind to come, and of course wheat, barley and corn. Others lived on orchards growing the biggest reddest apples, big as a babies head but far less ugly; then there were the pears, sweet and soft like a first love's kiss.

The wealthiest of them all, however, and somewhat set apart because of it, were those who lived on the livestock farms. Up to their knees in muck it was mystifying how they still managed to look down on us. They had the best land, the meadows closest to the rivers and streams ; lush pastures grazed throughout the warm weather while meadows full of flowers and tall grasses were left to grow high and lush until they were harvested to be dried for winter feed.

The life was hard, the days long but there was one thing above all others that worried the hamlets and villages dotted throughout: The Nervig!

These annoying little fey were responsible for stealing crops, fouling ponds and waterways and making milk go sour overnight even if stored inside a clay pot surrounded by cool water. It was commonplace to hear frazzled mothers saying to their children, 'If you ent careful you'll be taken by the Nervig, you mark my words if that ent the truth.'

To combat this threat was a network of old women who were known as the Ladies of the Six who claimed they were able to keep these pests quiescent. Their name came about due to a confusion between the language of the Mabhen and a local dialect in those parts that had all but died out some generations earlier. In Mabhen the word 'hex' means having to do with magic, particularly as it pertains to witchcraft, while in the old dialect 'hex' meant anything that was related to the number six. So the Ladies of Six were witches, wise women, or wicca women; at least that was the impression they liked to give.

The old ladies would travel around the farms painting hexes on barns, outbuildings, and houses. They would also bring bundles of dried plants tied into knots which they placed along tracks, tied to fences, or stuck on posts driven into the ground around the edges of fields. Naturally, in exchange for their services, they would receive a hearty meal, a basket or two of the produce from their patron and a payment in coin, this latter, though, being quite small as a rule because even a well-off farmer is not rich in money; their wealth being in land and what it produces.

The process by which a woman in the region became 'wise' upon reaching a certain age was one of the mysteries that lay beyond the ken of any outside their sorority. When not performing their functions they would usually coordinate to keep at least one day free per month for a get together. Had their patrons been able to see what happened during these communions they may have had cause to re-evaluate their relationship.

The main reason for these meetings was self-congratulatory in nature. They would each take it in turns to explain how good they had been at keeping a straight face when walking around with a bunch of old weeds. They would swap tips on different knots and what they should say they were good for. They would boast of their good fortune upon having received, say, a whole suckling pig or a gallon of barley wine. Then they would all sit down to a feast to which each would have contributed some of the largesse of their clients.

Lest you should think badly of these women you should note that in this region there was no need of a poor house, a stipend, or pension, whose costs would have to be levied through some form of tax. If there's one thing farmers have learned through the generations it is that if there is anything worse than a taxman they hope never to come across it.

Once

WENDY WOOLFSON

Once there was sugar coated
pastels in tubes, and
rainbow drops in toy shops,
the empty buildings filled
with freezing air, and feathers
whispering in your ears.
A sack full of dreams

All of it was silence, wind blowing,
whistling.
Her blank, stare-face
through cracked windows.

Wishes would fall, sad
sharp edged snowflakes,
into icy waters,
torn on the riptide.
Coloured candy, ashes on
the tongue.
No taste.

Now, you bring your
own sweet souls,
another time,
another place, and
what was once
terrible, becomes a gospel chant of choirs
in those tear-stained ears, singing
peace, love, and joy for
you have a boy and then another boy.

Angels Play Croquet

CHRIS TAIT

author of ''Diablo The Fantastical Adventures Of An Unloved Chess Piece'
and 'Diablo And The Leprechaun Figurehead'

Angels play croquet

Top hats are chimneys

Troughs of rain whisky

Scarecrows splash chutney

Pies cut by ploughmen

Cakes freeze to snowmen

Weddings with goblins

Tangled in bobbins

Beer barrels are bootleg

Wizard's eyes drip eggs

Diaries ripped to dregs

Mirror a witch nags

Ponds are like portraits

Snow is pearl gauntlets

Fountains of sherbet

Reel hares and rabbits

Ride in wheelbarrows

Over trench marrows

Secrets from the tarot

Whispered in furrows

Calendars take bows

The clocks are furloughed

With varnished meadows

Splintering burrows

Chalk fields are pillows

Antlers of willow

Candles are halos

Sheds share their shadows

Gladys

FIONA ANDERSON

Some pieces take you on a journey. They tell you a story and you share some of yours.

The Jacobean style dresser belongs to my friend. It had belonged to her late mother, Gladys, who purchased it many years ago before they emigrated to Australia. Like myself, the dresser is a British immigrant not designed for the semi-tropical climate of Queensland.

We had things in common from the get-go.

Loyalty to Gladys made my friend nervous to allow the dresser to be tampered with, but the dresser needed TLC. I offered suggestions for colour, style and finishes and my friend had it delivered to me, saying only 'My Mum liked green.'

The dresser had lived a life before I met her.

She was well travelled, with memories imprinted all over. Candle wax, cup stains, sticky-back plastic, cigarette burns, lost pennies, puppy teeth modifications and the accumulated tarnish we all gather when living a full life.

On first inspection, echoes of laughter and music spilled from her cupboards. I had visions of board games and children's artwork stacked next to a bottle of gin and one of sherry. Of hurried stuffing to hide homeless ephemera as the doorbell rang, announcing unexpected guests. The clanking of silver and Christmas carols could be heard as I opened the internal cutlery drawer. With that, memories of my own northern Christmases flooded my mind.

We were both familiar with the short, cold days and long, centrally heated nights. The gathering excitement of a bright day of celebration amongst a long-haul season of bleak days. The hustle in preparation of a day dedicated to mountains of torn paper, the obstacle course of children's discarded presents, of eating, drinking and food comas. Our shared experiences ended there.

As a child, I had anticipated a respite from the tyrant that posed as the perfect wife and mother for the benefit of Christmas guests. While she was otherwise occupied, I retreated to my mental cupboard away from the constant breath-holding awaiting the next blow, the undercurrent of fear that ruled my life. It was a place I knew well.

Christmas lights permanently dimmed when my nuclear family hit the shores of Australia. The blinding light and stifling heat of Christmas served only as a spotlight on our family dysfunction. No buffer of familial bodies, no festive fare and no reason to camouflage the truth for the outside world. My mental cupboard became ever deeper and darker as the years rolled by.

The dresser was delivered just in time for an old back injury to flare up, leaving me in excruciating pain. Murphy's Law. Anyone who suffers with chronic back pain will empathise with the fatigue, brain fog, inability to see straight and everything that comes with being in constant, terrible pain.

But I chipped away at Gladys' dresser as I could, using an office chair to wheel around the workshop for a few minutes at a time. It was a good distraction and a positive way to utilise my small reserves of energy.

It took me hours, days and weeks to strip, scrape, sand and clean the dresser inside and out. Using a razor blade, I scraped dirt and varnish away from her smallest corners. I hand sanded the beautiful turned legs and saw the significant cracks in her feet where the wood was parched.

As the layers of dust, dirt, wax, varnish and stain slowly faded away, the dresser started to breathe a sigh of relief as if I'd opened wide the curtains in a closed-up mansion that hadn't felt sunlight in its rooms for years. She needed help structurally too. Like a chiropractor for furniture, I knocked her backboard and shelves back into place which had fallen 2 inches from the weight of long held memories.

On occasion, Gladys herself came to visit. She stood looking over my shoulder with arms folded, mouth puckered and brow frowning. She regarded my efforts with reticence and doubt, withholding judgement until she could see the finished product.

Through my weeks of infrequent visits, the dresser and I formed a close bond. I played audio books while I worked, my hands being most creative when my ears focus on music or, in this case, a voice. The subject of the books was hard hitting with a surprising effect that provoked recollections of situations from my past; terrifying, painful experiences. Listening to the books, I rode an emotional rollercoaster as I learned, reflected and let go.

When waves of realisation and relief came upon me, the dresser drank my tears. With every scrape of paint stripper, every pass of sandpaper and every bucket of water, I released my pain and frustrations. She absorbed my maladies, drawing them into her rough oak grain where they dissolved and faded away, ever the stoic oak tree reminiscent of the crest of my family, standing sure.

She gave me moments of joy too. When I took to her handles with soap and steel wool, the green and black tarnish gave way to finely patterned brass. The engravings were beautifully worn by touch and time. I laughed with delight as they shone with a new vigour.

Our stories came together again at the moment I stripped the dresser from her last remnants of grime and varnish. Together we had released our pasts, keeping the best bits and banishing the bad.

What better way to celebrate her next chapter of life than with a new outfit and make-up? A coat of paint, a cap of stain, some rather lovely underwear in the form of fabric drawer and door liners, and hemp wax as lip gloss. She was ready to go home to my friend.

As for me, well, the morphine has given me relief as I wait the months til surgery. More so, the dresser and books have lifted the load that weighed heavily upon my back. I have deeper pockets of energy to follow the creative notions previously guarded in my mental cupboard.

I'll miss the dresser and our time together. And Gladys' visits. By the way, she highly approves of my work. After all, she does like green.

The Last Christmas

MARY TURNER THOMSON

author of 'The Bigamist' and 'The Psychopath'
'Trading Places' and 'The Sociopath Subtext'

I woke up on Christmas morning full of hope and joy. My husband was home for once – only the second Christmas he had spent with us in six years, and the sexy santa underwear (little triangles of red silk with white fluffly trim), had worked a treat the night before. As usual the 'smalls' (as my mother would refer to them) burst in en masse at 7am sharp. They had been told the day before not to attempt an awakening on Christmas Day on pain of presents being cancelled – this after the previous year of being woken at 4am after sitting up til 2am wrapping. An experience I did not want to repeat.

As the clock struck seven though, they were there – three of them bouncing on the bed and brandishing Santa's stockings which they would open together with us. This year there were two additional stockings – one for him and one for ME! Lush!

We were staying with my mum and dad – something that I always loved doing on Christmas – so breakfast was wonderful. Warm croissants, a pot of coffee. The smalls having cereal and juice. Sitting down together as a family and enjoying the excitement of the day to come – knowing that in the sitting room was a huge christmas tree (at least 7 ft tall) with SO many presents under it. With my three siblings joining us at lunchtime – along with their partners and 'smalls' - it was going to be a huge family day. Eighteen people in all and presents from each to the others already waiting under the tree. It was a veritable sparkly mountain and looked like something out of a Victorian picture book.

I loved that moment, Christmas breakfast, with the anticipation the day to come, of giving and receiving, of spending time together as a family. The games of Charades that we would play and how Mum – the lynchpin of our whole family – would make the whole day truly magical for us all. We finished breakfast and I sent the smalls off to get dressed whilst my husband and I helped mum with the clearing up – giving her a blank slate before the onslaught of cooking began.

Taking another cup of coffee from the depleted pot I went through to sit with the tree and admire the presents before the family descended. What I found though was utter carnage.

There was not one present left. The 'smalls' instead of going to get dressed had not been able to resist the pull of the tree. They were surrounded by an ocean of crumpled wrapping paper along with scarfs, candles, gadgets, games, chocolates and gifts galore. They had wild looks in their eyes, too far gone to even be afraid of a tellilng off – like junkies looking for the next high. They were digging through the paper trying to find more presents to open.

I coughed. They looked up and then back at the wrapping paper. Their mouths opened and closed again.

I just started to laugh.

So instead of unwrapping presents that Christmas we had a game of trying to remember who had bought what gift for whom. In some ways it was even more fun.

I don't remember specifically what any of the gifts were – it didn't really matter. What I do remember was the feast of good food, crackers, family, charades, wine and love. Mum humming Christmas hymns whilst cooking and smiling at all her grown up children and smalls around her. It was truly a feast for the soul.

It was the best Christmas I ever had, and it was also the last that my family was whole. Not because my 'husband' was deservedly jailed that year, but because my mother never made it to another. So a treasured memory and a lesson learnt – that the holidays are all about family and spending time together. Although we get tied up in thinking about the gifts we are buying, and what to get who, ultimately all that really matters - and all that will be remembered - is the love that we all share.

Printed in Great Britain
by Amazon